Lump TO Laughter

This book is the property of CREST Foundation (Cancer Research, Education, Support and Treatment). The revenue generated through this book will be used for cancer research activities and treatment of underprivileged patients. This foundation aims to bring down the burden of cancer in our society. We intend to increase awareness in women and help them in detecting this disease early, because when treatment is taken early, the chances of cure are very high.

For more information, visit **www.connectcrest.org** or reach us at 204 Gaana Apt, Yelachanahalli, JP Nagar, 6th Phase, Kanakapura Main Road, Bangalore – 78.

Lump TO Laughter

Breast Cancer...
It's time to talk

Dr. Jayanti S Thumsi

BLUEJAY

Bluejay Books Pvt. Ltd.
A-8/76, Ist Floor
Sector 16, Rohini
Delhi 110 085
info@bluejaybooksindia.com

First published by
Bluejay Books Pvt. Ltd. in 2015

Disclaimer: The book is designed to provide accurate and authoritative information in regard to the subject matter covered. It is meant to be a self-help book to spread awareness, and should not be considered as a substitute for your doctor's advice.

Printed and bound in India

Contents

Acknowledgements

Life is full of co-incidences, I think. Some people say whatever happens in our life is what is meant to happen. If I look back into my life, this book has been a very strange co-incidence.

I am a breast cancer surgeon practising in Bangalore for more than fifteen years. Like any typical surgeon, I too spent most of the years of my life in cutting and suturing. I thought that was all in my life.

In the year 2007, I did a course called Landmark Forum. It had a huge impact on me, as it enlightens you about your own self. In one of the Landmark sessions led by Mr. Rajendran (seminar leader of Landmark Worldwide and a well-known Bangalore builder), we as participants were asked to create what was possible for us in the future. I believe when one is ready, they just need a little push and encouragement to ignite their passion. Opportunity knocks the door of someone who is prepared. At that very moment, I exactly knew what I wanted to do in the future. With the help of my co-participants (Bhavesh Gupta and Shankar Narayanan Ganapathiraman), we designed "Lump to Laughter", an awareness program for early detection of breast cancer.

Breast cancer has carved a large niche for itself in cancer demographics and statistical data with its alarming rise. In my practice, I would often see a lot of women who came to us when the disease was already in an advanced stage. Many of them lost an opportunity to be completely cured because of lack of awareness, myths, ignorance, shyness and complacency. It pained me every time I saw a woman losing life, just because of lack of awareness. Breast cancer is one of the few cancers which can be completely cured, if detected and treated early. "Lump to Laughter" helps in creating that awareness in women.

Being a surgeon, I read many books, but never imagined that I could attempt to write one too. My colleague and friend Dr. Sachin Suresh Jadhav (Hematologist and Bone Marrow Transplant physician) once visited a bookstore at the Bangalore airport. He picked up a book on breast cancer meant for non-medical people, and found it not only uninspiring, but actually repulsive. He immediately called me to say that I need to write a book on this important topic. He explained that doing awareness programs had a very limited scope. Writing a book has a farther reach to the people and that makes a bigger difference. I instantly rejected the thought of it and in fact ridiculed him for having such an absurd and a preposterous idea. He not only tried to convince me but cajoled, pushed, forced, and unreasonably demanded me to write. He is a friend, philosopher and guide to many people. A task master by nature, he recognizes the potential in others and actually hand-holds and supports till the goal is achieved. I cannot thank him enough, as it is only because of him that this book is a reality today.

That's how my journey in writing began. There are so many people who have contributed to it. Sai Prasanna and Dr. Sandhya Kumar (my sisters-in-law), Dr. Shaibya Saldanha (co-founder, Enfold trust, my classmate at medical school and an awesome and a brilliant person. I have learnt so much from her and I always look up to her for support and guidance), and Mrs. Kamaldeep Peter (Senior program manager, Asia Pacific, Oracle Academy, my patient, a breast cancer survivor, a self-less person and someone who is ever ready to work for this cause) have helped me edit this book.

I thank all my patients and members of 'STHREE' who have enriched my life by allowing me to be a part of their healing process, whose stories I have incorporated in this book.

I am eternally grateful to my family and friends, specially my husband and my daughter for their unflinching support to me.

I dedicate this book to my mother Mrs. Vanaja Devasharma. She is an incredible person and an eternal source of inspiration to me. Although her education stopped after school and she had no opportunity to go to college, she is one of the wisest women that I have ever known in my life. She is an epitome of unconditional love, contribution, optimism, persistence and patience. Her pride and faith in me has been the source of my energy and my existence.

I thank my classmate Dr. Niraj Rathod, who has been very supportive. He has made the whole process seem very easy for me.

My beloved teachers and world renowned physician Dr. O.P. Kapoor and surgeon Dr. Tempton Udwadia have trained and inspired not just me, but thousands of students like me who in turn have become stalwarts in their fields. Whatever I am today is only because of the basic training I received in Grant Medical College, JJ Group of hospitals, Mumbai.

This book is the property of CREST Foundation (Cancer Research, Education, Support and Treatment). The revenue generated through this book will be used for cancer research activities and treatment of underprivileged patients. This foundation aims to bring down the burden of cancer in our society. We intend to increase awareness in women and help them in detecting this disease early, because when treatment is taken early, the chances of cure are very high.

I thank all the trustees of our foundation (Dr. Sachin Jadhav, Mrs. Sujatha Bharadwaj, and Ms. Neeta Jadhav). Their solidarity with me has made this book possible.

This book is an account of the journey of women with breast cancer and their emotions during different phases of treatment. It narrates my experience with my patients with medically validated information and the stories of women who have gone beyond their fear to become cancer survivors. I wanted to share with the world new cancer conquering stories that weave the science of medicine and the philosophy of experience into one cohesive fabric. When you read the book, I ambitiously hope to deliver hope, inspiration, information, support and optimistic reality for those who seek it.

Most importantly, this is a documentation of my life's precious learnings. And I think learning is always meant to be shared.

Foreword

Dr. Jayanti Thumsi was my student at Grant Medical College from 1984 onwards, completing her post-graduation in surgery in 1993. At JJ Hospital, there is an ethos of constant inquiry into one's work and a need to strive towards perfection in one's skills. Jayanti has developed both in abundance with more than fifteen years of surgical experience in Mumbai and Bangalore.

In the present scenario of health in India, breast cancer is rearing its ugly head as the most common cancer in urban women. But the tragedy of this disease is that while early detection and effective management can drastically reduce morbidity and mortality, lack of awareness in the public domain prevents women from seeking early and correct treatment.

Through this book Dr. Jayanti Thumsi has tried to bridge this huge lacuna. In the simplest language and through the narratives of her patients, she has brought an emotionally complex medical issue into comprehensible steps of detection and care. She has given statistical details of incidences and enumerated the signs and symptoms of breast cancer. The screening procedures have been listed in great detail which a lay person may follow with confidence. Her various caveats to patients on the dos and don'ts as well as her encouraging words will bring succor to the reader, whether sufferer or family members. While she emphasizes the need for vigilance and prompt action, she brings positivity to the discourse and underlines the need for a holistic approach.

She is invited to international fora to discuss her management. While she is using her surgical expertise and team approach to treat huge number of patients, she is seeking to collate data about the specifics of breast cancer in Indian women to improve both detection and survival.

She has a deeply compassionate approach and a determination to alleviate her patients suffering in the most effective way. This book is a small step towards her goals. My best wishes to Dr. Jayanti.

Dr O P Kapoor
Senior consultant Physician,
Eminent physician, a prolific author,
and a gifted teacher who has been
teaching medicine for the past 61 years.

The lump

ᴧ

It was a busy out-patient clinic, just like any other day. We were working nonstop after finishing two surgeries. There was some unusual chaos in the out-patient department (OPD). Somebody seemed very agitated and I came out of my consultation room to see what the matter was. There was a woman weeping inconsolably, and her husband was requesting the receptionist to allow her to consult us out of turn. Seeing their tense faces, I knew we had to see them even without an appointment.

Divya was a forty-two-year-old, educated, smart, and well-read lady. She walked into my OPD with a tense expression, and an equally tense husband. Someone had directed her to consult our team and as I gathered next, it was time she did! She had noticed a lump in her breast six months back. Like many people, she was too busy to see a doctor immediately.

Strange, isn't it? We are all, often, too busy to notice changes in our bodies. We fail to realise the significance of seemingly trivial bodily changes. And we avoid taking steps to stall the progress or onset of diseases.

Divya, being a professional, had no time to seek immediate medical help. She was a software engineer, who had pending work, responsibilities, deadlines to meet and targets to achieve at the office. Only after three months, she took time out to see a gynaecologist, who promptly asked her to undergo a mammogram. The mammogram was reported as "Left breast lump which looks noncancerous..." The gynaecologist reassured her that it was a benign lump, and not cancerous..

This put her misgivings to rest and her busy life continued, and so did the growth of that seemingly benign lump. The mass kept growing in size and her anxiety grew with it. The persistent anxiety in her mind made her see another gynaecologist. That was when she was referred to us.

Do I need to see a breast cancer surgeon?

In our society, women would rather not go to any doctor for the fear of being diagnosed with some deadly disease. You can imagine what would be the predicament if they were referred to a breast cancer surgeon. Absolutely terrifying!

I examined Divya, and clinically it did seem like a cancerous lump. We immediately reviewed her previous mammogram with a team of experienced radiologists. The suspicion grew.

A delayed diagnosis once again!

Three crucial months lost! I felt frustrated at the thought of losing the opportunity to treat her earlier and improving the chances for a complete cure. That is what I regretted.

On further enquiry, I also learnt that her mother was treated for cancer of the breast at the age of sixty. I wondered whether the genes had come to play their role in Divya's case.

She was worried, and at the same time, disturbing thoughts were running in my mind too.

Role of a woman

A woman is a beautiful creation. No short of a marvel! She is a daughter, sister, wife, mother, daughter-in-law, friend and a soul mate. She is a one (wo-)man army holding many fronts at home and work. You must have seen her effortlessly oscillating between the roles of a cook, homemaker, employee, manager, or a boss. She can endure, persist, and stand up to hardships of life and smile, all at the same time, and her caring and sharing nature stands out. Her commitment, responsibility and love for her family and near and dear ones is unmatched.

As the saying goes: 'If you educate a girl, you educate the entire generation'. Similarly, 'When a woman's health is taken care of, the entire family is taken care of'.

My family, my first priority!

Everyone else, everything else seems to be more important for a woman than her needs, including her own health. Why is it that even her health always takes a back seat? This question always haunts me. I see that women, even the educated and accomplished ones, are so negligent. Is it lack of awareness or is it that they are so indifferent that they do not even care for themselves? Are they so caught up in juggling between home and work that they have lost the connection with their own being? Who is to be blamed? Is it the husband, the family, the boss at work, her career, or herself?

There have been reports that the majority of women in India, including those in urban areas, visit their doctor when their disease is in an advanced stage, making cure difficult. This is a harsh reality.

I am convinced that education and awareness are two different things. A woman may be highly qualified, but that she is also aware, may not be true. Be it a woman from urban or rural area or any socioeconomic strata, self-denial, lack of awareness and lack of health consciousness in Indian women is a stark reality. An alarming majority of women, including the urban-educated ones, come to the doctor when their fears are too huge to be quelled. Are we all so caught up and consumed by daily existence that we have lost the bigger picture of life?

These thoughts resurfaced in my mind after meeting Divya, who had many more questions to ask.

Some more tests... really?

ꕤ

'But I already had a mammogram which was very painful. They compressed my breast. Do I really need more tests?' This was Divya's query.

I replied, 'Sure mammograms are painful, but so is waxing the arms and shaping up of the eyebrows!'

A mammogram to-date is the single most effective screening investigation. It can pick up very small abnormalities which cannot be felt even by a doctor's skilled fingers. The smaller the size of the tumour at the beginning of the treatment, the better the outcome. As the tumour grows in size, so do the challenges. The mammogram helps us in detecting the tumour when it is still tiny and just a few millimetres in size.

With early stage breast cancer, there is often no lump to be felt, but the mammogram can detect small areas of calcium deposits in patterns within the breast tissue. These are called calcifications. They can develop in both cancerous and non cancerous diseases of the breast. However, even amongst the lumps that are felt, 80% are non-cancerous.

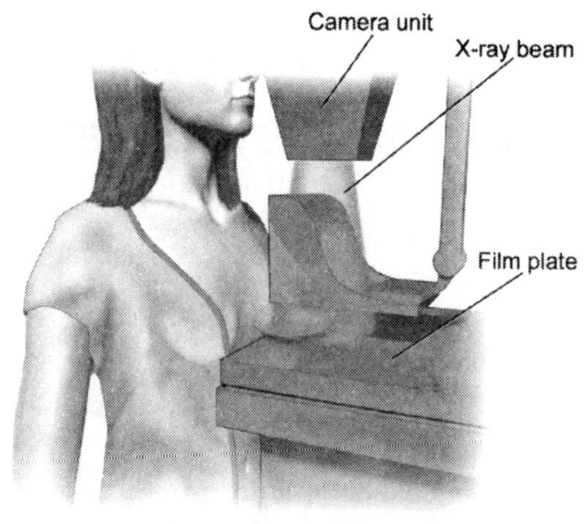

Figure 1: How a mammogram works.

A biopsy is the investigation which can tell us whether the abnormality is malignant or not. It is a test wherein a needle is introduced at the site of the tumour. A small tissue or fluid is removed from the suspicious area and the morphology of the cells is studied under the microscope. This test aids us in planning further treatment for the patient.

A biopsy can also be of three types – FNAC (Fine needle aspiration cytology), a core biopsy, or a surgical biopsy. FNAC is practically painless and can be performed in the outpatient clinic. A core biopsy is performed under local anaesthesia, but does not require admission. In primary care centres, a surgical biopsy is done under general anaesthesia to obtain a histo pathological diagnosis. In tertiary care centres, this procedure is combined with further definitive surgical management at the same sitting to reduce health risks and costs to the patient.

Divya had to wait for two days to get the biopsy report. She was terribly anxious; the family members repeatedly called us to know the diagnosis.

One of the most difficult things for a doctor to do, is to break *the news*. Once again, I had to confront an uncomfortable situation.

In my opinion, every patient, educated or not, should be told about the diagnosis and the treatment options in detail and complete clarity. This would help them make an informed choice. It is each person's right to know and understand the disease that their body is gripped with.

Families frequently request doctors to hide the diagnosis from the patient. In fact, by not informing her, we are underestimating her power and strength to deal with the situation. We are also depriving her of the right to make choices for her own body.

Do I really have cancer?

The word cancer is shocking and disturbing in itself. It feels like it's the end of the world, as if there is no tomorrow.

Divya was shocked. Why *me*? There was a blank expression on her face.

She said, 'But I feel fit. Oh, it can't happen to me. I have done no wrong. I have not caused harm to anyone. My lifestyle is very simple. God can't punish me like this.' Endless questions and endless thoughts arising from shock and denial. Denial cannot help for sure.

I had to be extremely patient to understand Divya's fears and concerns. I have seen that patients who have a good family support can deal with their situation better, as compared to women who are devoid of it.

'Doctor, I want to live. I have a small child. I have lots of responsibilities at home,' was her overarching anxiety.

Fear of death can be unnerving, but the desire to live for someone you love, either a child or your spouse or any other person, can give you enormous courage to face it head on and go through the treatment.

I feel the first step to deal with this situation is awareness. And the second step is acceptance. It can help in coping with the consequences of any misfortune.

Is cancer such a bad word?

We are no longer in the 18th century, when it would be called an incurable disease.

Cancer can often be cured. Breast cancer is one of the few cancers which is completely curable, if detected and treated early.

The data analysis of the follow-up of over two years in our department showed a survival rate of more than 90%. This included patients of different age groups, with different types, and stages of the disease. This is achievable only if every patient undergoes meticulous assessment, appropriately tailored treatment and stringent follow ups.

There have been rapid strides in the medical field. Today, there are lots of treatment options and advanced surgical techniques available to reach this goal.

Surgery, chemotherapy, radiotherapy, and hormone therapy are various modalities of treatment available. We evaluate patients and then decide the best option for them.

Among the various tests which were done for Divya was a PET-CT scan (Positron Emission Tomography). It scans the whole body. We can precisely stage the disease with it. This means that we can find out how much the cancer has spread.

An injection with a substance made up of sugar and a small amount of radioactive material is given. Cancer cells tend to be more active than normal cells. They absorb more of the radioactive sugar as a result. A special camera picks up these cells in different sites of the body and enables us to know if the cancer has spread to other organs.

God! How do I deal with this disease and its treatment?!

Divya was introduced to one of the volunteers of STHREE.

STHREE is an organisation which Supports to Heal, Restore, Empower and Energize patients who are undergoing treatment for breast cancer. It is an organisation of like-minded people, some of whom are cancer patients and cancer survivors. The family members of cancer survivors, the medical fraternity, and the patients' well-wishers also participate in its activities.

The volunteer who supported Divya was a breast cancer survivor herself. She had successfully completed the treatment and was leading a normal and healthy life.

'What do I do now? Will I lose my hair? Isn't the treatment prolonged and painful? Do I have to go through all of this?' Divya asked the STHREE volunteer.

There is a lot of relief in speaking to someone who has gone through the treatment herself. Familiarity can also breed comfort sometimes. It gave Divya a ray of hope.

Will I lose my femininity?

'Will you remove my breast to free me of the disease? Will I lose my femininity? How will I face the world?' Divya's mind was abuzz with doubts and questions and it was necessary to help her understand what her body was to go through.

'Well, not really Divya. Ideally, we should have operated on you six months ago, when the lump was first noticed. However, the lump is still reasonably small. We can perform a breast conservation surgery.'

'Doctor, but is it safe for me to undergo the breast conservation surgery? Will the cancer not recur? Isn't it better that my entire breast is removed?' was her dilemma.

There is much advancement in breast cancer treatment. Newer and more effective treatment options are now available.

Two main types of surgeries are performed for the treatment of breast cancer – Breast conservation surgery and complete mastectomy.

Breast conservation surgery can now be offered to most women. Only the cancerous lump in the breast and a small amount of surrounding normal tissue is removed. The rest of the breast tissue is left intact. There have been many studies which have shown that breast conservation surgery followed by radiation therapy is as effective and safe as complete removal of the breast.

The second option is complete mastectomy, where the affected breast is fully removed. In these cases, reconstruction surgeries can be done in the same sitting as the main surgery.

Our body is primarily the medium for our identity. The moment we are told that a portion of our body is going to change in its appearance, we become apprehensive as it directly affects our identity and how we perceive ourselves. Medical advancement has ensured that the woman can retain her femininity and continue to identify with her body after surgery, through breast reconstruction.

Reconstruction surgery creates an artificial breast. This is a procedure that allows for the immediate rebuilding of the breast of the patient. A new breast mound is created which is of similar size and shape as the original breast. The surgical technique is so sophisticated now that the reconstructed breast is close to real. Such a reconstruction surgery can either be implant-based or autologous (using the patient's own tissue).

All these surgeries are time tested and very safe.

I always encourage women to look beyond the diagnosis and treatment of cancer. They should look forward to getting cured and to leading a full life as cancer survivors. We can now focus not only on clearing cancer from their body, but also preventing them from feeling incomplete as women.

I am too scared to be on the operation table

The morning of the surgery arrived. Divya refused to be shifted into the operation theatre. Before the surgery, she wanted to vent out her feelings.

I admit that as doctors we get so mechanised that we sometimes become oblivious of the human touch. Before going into the operation theatre for Divya's surgery, I had to finish seeing some patients who were waiting for their consultation in our outpatient clinic. There were some who had come from far off places. So I rushed into the operation theatre as quickly as I could. Divya was waiting for me.

One look at her and I could guess what she was going through. Her eyes met mine. It felt like she was pouring her heart out to me. She seemed to be pleading for help to get her out of this situation. I could see the fear in her eyes, but I could also sense her immense trust in us. She had surrendered herself. How could one not be moved by her feelings? I held her hand and reassured her that we would do our best to get her out of this disease.

I promised her that our entire team would be with her to make her treatment as easy as possible. It calmed her down and gave her some courage to face the knife.

Is the treatment over after surgery?

Divya's final biopsy report clearly indicated stage 2 disease. The next step was to go through chemotherapy. She was devastated. 'Doctor, you said that the surgery has gone well, the entire tumour has been removed. So why do I need chemotherapy?'

'When we do the surgery, we can remove the abnormality that our eyes can see. That is we can remove the "gross" disease. But very often, there is what is called as micro metastasis. There could still be a spread of the disease which is microscopic at this point of time; which means that there is a possibility that the small cancer cells could still be circulating all over the body. These cells are so small that our eyes cannot see them, nor can they be detected by any scan. If we do not manage these cells now, then there are chances that they will grow and later create tumours in some other organ of the body. The only way to kill these cells is by giving chemotherapy.'

She was listening intently, but her face still showed worry. I continued, 'Chemotherapy consists of certain kinds of injections and occasionally oral medicines. When given intravenously, they travel throughout the body via our blood and they have the potential to kill the cancer cells. It prevents cancer cells from growing and spreading by destroying the cells or stopping them from dividing.

'Cancer cells tend to grow and divide very quickly, with no order or control. Because they're growing so fast, sometimes these cells break away from the original tumour and travel to other places in the body. Chemotherapy weakens and destroys cancer cells at the original tumour site and throughout the body.

'Chemotherapy is often given as a day care procedure, usually once in three weeks. Though the regime may differ for each patient, a person may need four to eight cycles of chemotherapy depending on the type of cancer, age of the patient and many such factors,' I explained.

'I will lose my hair, my periods will stop, and a part of my breast has already been removed. I will have nothing of a woman left in me,' was her concern.

I put her fears to rest and told her, 'Most normal cells grow and divide in a precise, orderly way. But some cells divide rapidly, for example cells in hair follicles, nails, the mouth, digestive tract, and bone marrow. Chemotherapy unintentionally harms these other types of rapidly dividing cells, causing various side effects. These side effects can be hairfall, darkening of nails, vomiting, diarrhoea, gastritis, frequent coughs and colds and anaemia (due to bone marrow depression).

'Sure, chemotherapy is a difficult phase, but most of the side effects are temporary. They usually last only as long as you are taking the treatment. Once you finish the treatment, your hair will grow back. Until such time, you can get a wig made for yourself. Professional wig makers will be willing to help you. They can make a wig out of your own hair or by using artificial hair. And nowadays these are really good!' The aesthetic support for cancer patients is far more advanced and patient specific than ever before.

This brought a smile to Divya's face. She understood that there seemed to be a solution to most of the side effects. She felt very hopeful and was ready to go through the next phase of the treatment.

Why only me?

It is easy to make friends with the other patients in the chemotherapy ward. Divya could relate to Preeti and they seemed comforted in each other's presence. Preeti had a very interesting story to share. She was a thirty-two-year-old divorcee. She was a teacher by profession and had an eight-year-old child. She was diagnosed to have stage 3 breast cancer.

Preeti had undergone breast MRI (Magnetic Resonance Imaging) and a needle biopsy for the diagnosis of her tumour. She was told that a mammogram was not of much use in women below the age of forty years. A woman's breast is very dense before forty years of age and hence a mammogram may not give all the information that we are looking for. Breast MRI may be a better investigation for younger women. Thus, she was advised a breast MRI.

MRI scans use magnets and radio waves instead of x rays to produce very detailed, cross sectional images of the body. Very often, a contrast material called Gadolinium is injected into the blood vessel before or during the test. This improves the ability of the MRI to clearly show breast tissue details.

Unfortunately, in Preeti's case, it had shown a multicentric disease which meant that in addition to the main tumour, she had small deposits of the cancer cells in all the quadrants (parts) of the breast.

Luckily, the PET-CT did not show any evidence of the disease having spread to any other distant organ like liver, lungs, bones, and brain. She had already taken three cycles of neoadjuvant chemotherapy.

This type of chemotherapy is given even before the surgery to make the tumour smaller in size, and hence easier to remove. After three cycles of this, she had undergone complete removal of the breast (mastectomy). But luckily, she had various options for breast reconstruction.

Preeti chose breast reconstruction using an implant. Many safe and good quality implants are available now. She had opted for the latest variety of the implant which was a onetime procedure. When her breast was removed, this permanent implant was put in to replace it during the same surgery. From her appearance, nobody could even make out that she had undergone a complete removal of the breast. The implant was shaped just like her natural breast and her appearance was flawlessly original.

Preeti was a fun-loving, warm lady. Humour was a part of her conversation and every sentence was full of it. She could laugh at herself and make fun of anybody and everybody. The lighter side of life actually shone brightly in Preeti's presence. She was the star of the chemotherapy ward. Everybody seemed to be waiting to meet her, listen to her jokes and her witty comments. Divya and Preeti seemed to have become best of friends.

During Divya's second chemotherapy, there was a new admission in the chemotherapy ward. It was Ameena, a twenty-eight-year-old Iraqi lady who had developed a breast lump during her third pregnancy.

She had noticed this lump during the fifth month of her pregnancy and a Trucut needle or core biopsy had proven this to be malignant. In fact, her entire right breast had turned into a cancerous lump. Ameena had a condition called inflammatory cancer of the breast. She had heard about our hospital and travelled all the way from Baghdad to India. She was given an option of continuing the pregnancy in spite of the cancer, but she chose otherwise. A PET-CT scan, which was done in our hospital six months ago, had unfortunately shown that the disease had already spread to her bones.

On admission to the ward, Ameena looked very sceptical and worried. She did not know anybody, nor did she know the language. She seemed very timid, clinging on to her husband who was an engineer working in Baghdad, Iraq. The only way one could communicate with her was through a translator.

Divya had decided to put her at ease. She initiated a conversation with her with the help of Ali, who was an Arabic translator. Ameena and her husband Abdul were concerned only about the well-being of their family. Isn't it strange that human beings from any part of the world are very similar? Human sentiments are really the same on any side of the equator. All that everybody wants is safety and good health for their family and a peaceful and happy life. Ameena and Abdul were no different. They were concerned about their two little children, whom they had left back at their home in Iraq.

She took the first cycle of chemotherapy in our hospital and then subsequent five cycles in her own country. She had returned to our hospital after six months and was admitted for evaluation and also to know the response to the six cycles of chemotherapy which she had already received. She was scheduled for a PET-CT scan.

It seemed like result time for her. She was nervous and did not know what was in store for her. Divya's presence was a big relief for her. They seemed to communicate even without knowing each other's language. They were able to understand each other merely by being together.

I am strong enough to support others

By the time Divya had finished her fourth cycle of chemotherapy, she seemed to have become confident to share her experiences with other patients. Divya and some patients had formed a group of their own, a support structure of their own. They had their WhatsApp group and a Gmail group. Messages and emails were being exchanged on regular basis. Homemade solutions for some of the chemotherapy side effects were shared. They were motivating each other, supporting and helping each other through one of the most difficult phases of their lives. We were touched by their bonding. I believe there is more joy in giving and sharing. When you focus on contributing to others or on healing others, your body automatically seems to heal. All our patients seemed to have heightened energy levels when they went through their treatment together.

By evening, Ameena's PET-CT report was ready and it was very encouraging. Thanks to all the chemotherapy drugs, there was no trace of the disease anywhere in her body, except for a small residual lump in her breast. She was overjoyed. Tears of happiness were rolling down her cheeks. All the other patients and the staff of the ward were happy for her. They all seemed like one big family, supporting and encouraging each other. I was overwhelmed to see their unity. Now we had only to tackle the remnant in the breast.

A new woman

I noticed a complete change in Divya's personality by the time she had finished her sixth cycle, the last chemotherapy. She seemed calm, composed and to have accepted the situation. Her posture, her body language had transformed into one of strength and confidence.

Divya was now bald and wearing a wig. Even her eyebrows and eye lashes had vanished. Her nails were black in colour and she had dark circles around her eyes. She seemed weak, fragile and tired, yet she looked beautiful to my eyes. She looked very happy. I was amazed to see the change in her. I wanted to know what made her so happy. What she then shared with me was very enriching to me, even personally.

'Doctor, I went through different phases of emotions since the time of my diagnosis. I was in denial, I was angry with my body, angry with god, angry with my circumstances. I had resisted the treatment, it caused me pain and it hurt me. I thought life was not fair, that I was being punished for no fault of mine.

'I have to admit, I always knew anyone could be diagnosed with cancer, even me. But like so many women, I never thought it would actually be me someday. I never thought that I would have to hear those devastating words: "You have breast cancer."

'But when I was admitted in the hospital, I met other patients. I saw the suffering of others. I saw children suffering. There were patients with no family to support them. There were those who had no money to pay for their treatment. Some had travelled considerable distances to get the treatment which was so easily available to me. Then there were others with a more advanced disease than mine.'

I was smiling to hear her confident words, so she continued with a smile, 'I realised that life is a package deal. It comes with a set of happiness and also a set of challenges. Life is not perfect. I may not have a choice all the time, I may not be able to choose my circumstances all the time, but I realised that I had a choice to choose my reaction to a particular situation. I had a choice to either sit or lament over my situation and my misfortune, or choose to go through the treatment and thus give myself a chance to get cured of the disease. Life is not what it's supposed to be. It is what it is. The way you cope with it is what makes the difference. You can be a victim of cancer, or a survivor of cancer. It's a mindset.

'I thought of Martin Luther King Jr's quote: "We must accept finite disappointment, but never lose infinite hope." After all, everything that is done in the world is done through hope. I understood that only if I face the sun, will the shadows fall behind.

'I realised that no doctor, no medicines can cure me without my cooperation. I had an inexplicable fear of surgery and chemotherapy, but I decided to choose courage. After all, courage is not the absence of fear; it is about taking necessary actions in the face of fear. Courage is the triumph over fear. A brave person is not one who does not feel scared, but one who continues in spite of that fear. No one is necessarily born with courage, but one is born with the potential ability to face any situation. Life shrinks or expands in proportion to one's courage. I chose courage.

'Is womanhood only about breast, hair, nails, and ovaries? I realised there was much more to it than these superficial attributes. True womanhood is about our qualities. It is about caring, compassion, courage, love, sharing, contributing, and achieving our true potential. It is about generating happiness and peace, and not just passively waiting and hoping for miracles to happen. It is about taking charge of our life and it is not just about blaming others or blaming circumstances and thus succumbing to fate.'

I was amazed by the change in her attitude. Adversities can sometimes be blessings in disguise. It often brings out the best in a person. It actually reveals a person's true character. I felt so proud of her.

No wonder she looked so beautiful and radiant. She had accessed her inner beauty.

Will I be judged?

Divya had decided to restart work at her office while her radiation regime was on.

Radiation therapy is another form of treatment where local control of the disease is achieved by utilizing high-energy waves such as x-rays to kill cancer cells. With the advanced radiation machines which are available these days, the radiation that is given to the affected area can be very precise and accurate. 3D models of the tumour are created and also of the surrounding normal structures. This facilitates radiation therapy to be focused only on the tumour. It kills only the targeted cancerous cells, but the normal surrounding tissue can be spared as far as possible from the radiation, thus decreasing the short term and long term side effects.

These high-energy beams, which are invisible to the human eye, damage a cell's DNA, the material that the cells use to divide. The radiation damages all the cells that are in the path of its beam. It kills normal cells as well as cancer cells. But radiation affects cancer cells more than normal cells. Cancer cells grow and multiply very fast. These two activities can be slowed or stopped by radiation damage. And because cancer cells are less organized than healthy cells, it's harder for them to repair the damage done by radiation. So cancer cells are more easily destroyed by radiation, while healthy, normal cells are better able to repair themselves and survive the treatment.

Some people do fear radiation therapy, but the radiation used in cancer treatment is highly focused, controllable, and generally safe.

Divya's first day at work was quite difficult. She was scared of being judged, of people being too sympathetic to her. She was very conscious about her looks, her physical condition. As she started working, her confidence levels rose. She continued to visit the hospital daily for radiation. During this time, she was more than happy to help anybody around. While she was supporting others, she started asking new questions.

'Will the cancer recur?' This was a nagging thought at the back of her mind.

What if it comes back?

Follow up after cancer therapy is as important as the treatment itself. Periodical follow up with certain set of investigations is absolutely essential. In case of a recurrence, it helps in detecting it at an early stage.

Irrespective of whether it is a recurrence or the primary disease, it is easier to treat it when it is detected early. However, the chances of recurrence depend largely on the type and the stage of the disease.

Among the patients who are diagnosed early, i.e. in stage 1 or 2, more than 85% of patients get cured. On the other hand, in patients with stage 4 disease, the chances of getting better are much less.

Cancer that is localised to the breast has a better prognosis as compared to that which has grown beyond the breast and to the lymph nodes. Especially if the spread has already occured to the other organs (stage 4 disease), the prognosis is the poorest.

Hence the key is to detect the disease early.

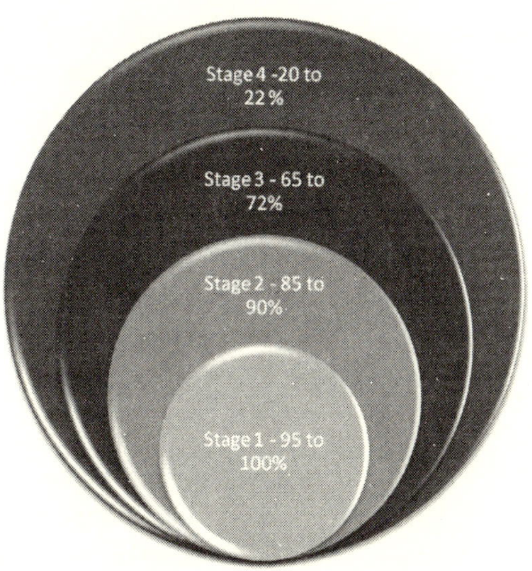

Figure 2: Five year survival rate in different stages of the disease.

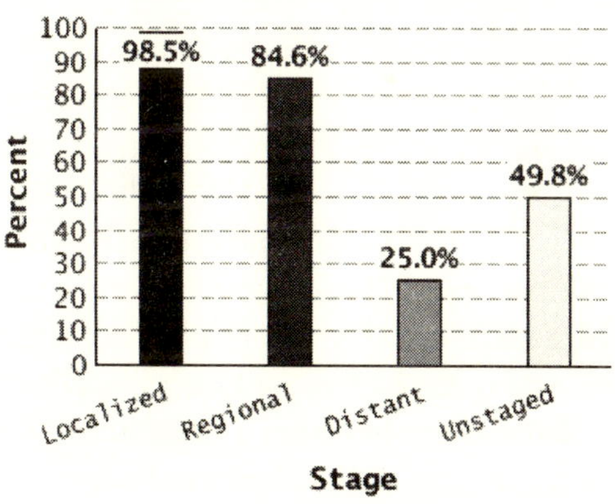

Figure 3: Five year survival rate for breast cancer.

The earlier we detect the disease, the easier is the treatment and less radical surgeries will be required. In these cases, breast conservation surgeries can be performed. In many of these patients, even chemotherapy may not be required. This could decrease the cost and duration of treatment, and most importantly, the chances of cure are very high.

According to the WHO report in the USA, in 2012, approximately 2.32 lakh women were estimated to be diagnosed to have breast cancer, but only 44,000 (18%) patients died because of the disease in the same year. Whereas in India, approximately 1.45 lakh women were estimated to be diagnosed with breast cancer in 2012, and 70,000 (48%) of patients were estimated to have died due to it.

So in the USA, about 1 in 5 or 6 women diagnosed with this disease succumb, but in our country, 1 in 2 women do not survive. This happens because women in western countries consult the doctor at an early stage; whereas in our country, women approach doctors only when the disease is at an advanced stage.

Most developed countries understand the importance of routine health check-ups. Hence, even if more number of women are detected with breast cancer in the USA, the number of deaths due to this disease are much less as compared to the women in India.

Collectively, US, India and China account for almost one-third of the global breast cancer burden. Persistent efforts over last forty to fifty years in the US have resulted in a large proportion of women presenting themselves for timely consultations in early stages. As a result, there has been a consistent decrease in the death rates, even though the incidence of breast cancer is rising steadily. The chart that follows shows the estimated figures of breast cancer cases, deaths and prevalence across the world in the year 2012.

GLOBOCAN 2012: Estimated Cancer Incidence, Mortality and Prevalence Worldwide in 2012

International Agency for Research on Cancer

Estimated numbers (thousands)	Cases	Deaths	5-year prev.
World	1671	522	6232
More developed regions	788	198	3201
Less developed regions	883	324	3032
WHO Africa region (AFRO)	100	49	318
WHO Americas region (PAHO)	408	92	1618
WHO East Mediterranean region (EMRO)	99	42	348
WHO Europe region (EURO)	494	143	1936
WHO South-East Asia region (SEARO)	240	110	735
WHO Western Pacific region (WPRO)	330	86	1276
IARC membership (24 countries)	935	257	3591
United States of America	233	44	971
China	187	48	697
India	145	70	397
European Union (EU-28)	362	92	1444

Figure 4: Breast cancer cases, deaths and prevalence across the world in the year 2012.

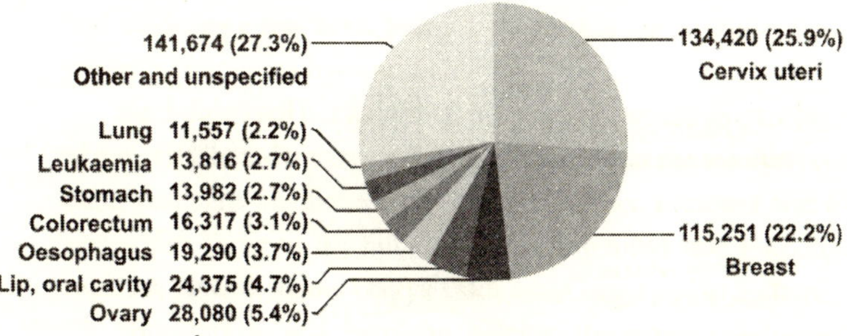

Figure 5: Incidence of types of cancer in India in 2008.

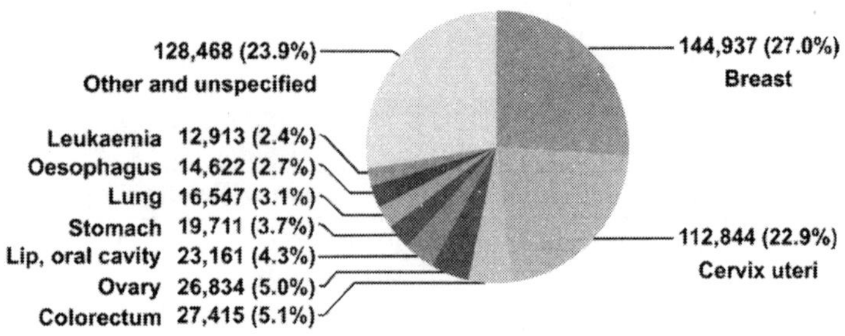

Figure 6: Incidence of types of cancer in India in 2012.

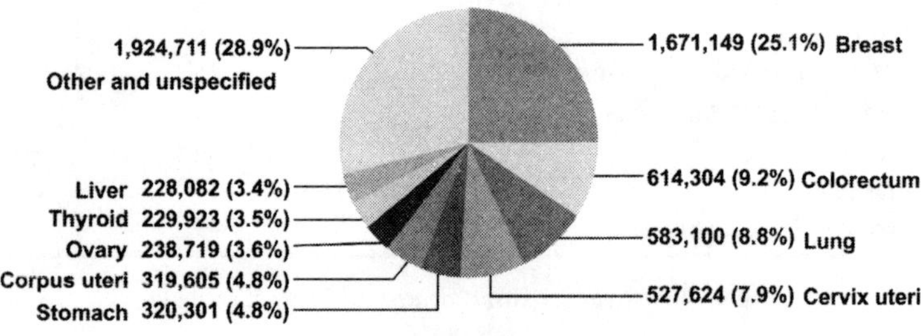

Figure 7: Incidence of types of cancer across the world in 2012.

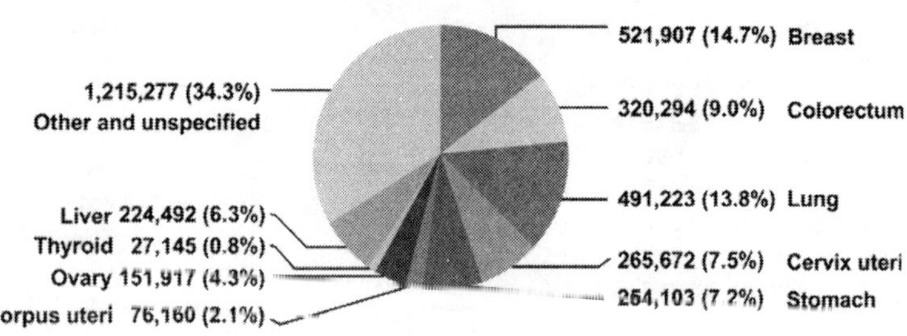

Figure 8: Morality owing to different types of cancer across the world in 2012.

For the United States, in the year 2012:

- 232,714 women were detected with breast cancer
- 43,909 women died of breast cancer
- 232714 / 43909 = 5.29 = round it off to 5 or 6.

So roughly, in the US, for every 5 or 6 women diagnosed with breast cancer, one woman is dying of it.

For India, in the year 2012:

- 144,937 women we detected with breast cancer
- 70,218 women died of breast cancer
- 144937 / 70218 = 2.06 = round it off to 2.

So roughly, in India, for every 2 women diagnosed with breast cancer, one woman is dying of it.

WHO prediction for cancer in India

Let's consider the following table, wherein one can see the number of cases with reference to two dominant age bands as per WHO (World Health Organization).

Year	Estimated number of new cancers (all ages)	Male	Female	Both sexes
2012		-	144937	-
	ages < 65	-	125245	-
	ages >= 65	-	19692	-
2015		-	155863	-
	ages < 65	-	134006	-
	ages >= 65	-	21857	-
	Demographic change	-	10926	-
	ages < 65	-	8761	-
	ages >= 65	-	2165	-

Figure 9: Number of breast cancer cases in India in 2015, as against 2012.

Similarly, the table that follows shows deaths owing to breast cancer in the year 2015, as against 2012, with respect to two major age-band divisions.

Year	Estimated number of new cancers (all ages)	Male	Female	Both sexes
2012		-	70218	-
	ages < 65	-	53480	-
	ages >= 65	-	16738	-
2015		-	75957	-
	ages < 65	-	57373	-
	ages >= 65	-	18584	-
	Demographic change	-	5739	-
	ages < 65	-	3893	-
	ages >= 65	-	1846	-

Figure 10: Number of deaths owing to breast cancer in India in 2015, as against 2012.

The Population forecasts were extracted from the United Nations, World Population Prospects, the 2012 revision.
Numbers are computed using age-specific rates and corresponding populations for ten age-groups.

Let us now see IARC, WHO (International Agency for Research on Cancer, World Health Organization) predictions for India in 2015 with respect to incidence and mortality specifically in breast cancer cases.

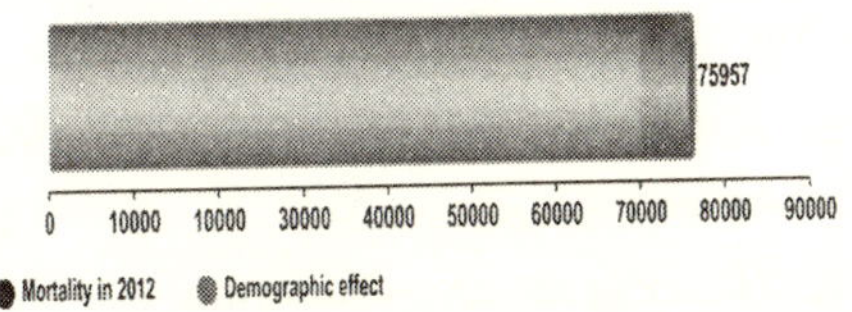

Figure 11: Number of predicted deaths due to different types of cancer across ages in 2105.

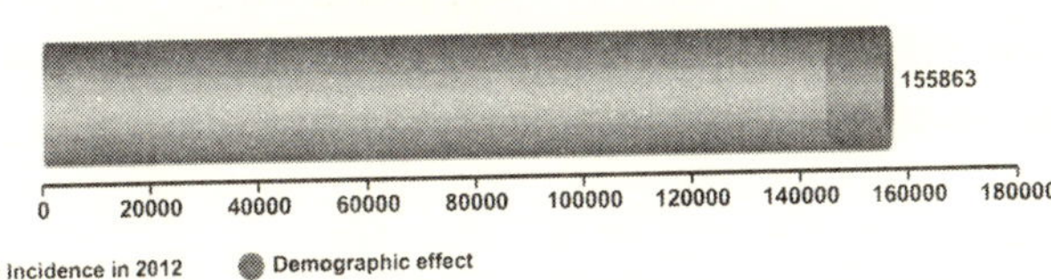

Figure 12: Number of predicted new cancer cases across ages in 2105.

Figures 11 and 12 show the prediction of numbers of deaths due to breast cancer in 2015 and the predictions of the numbers of newly-detected cases of breast cancer.

For the years 2015, there will be an estimated 1,55,000 new cases of breast cancer and about 76,000 women in India are expected to die of the disease. The gap only seems to be widening, which means, we need to work aggressively on early detection.

The Lancet[1] journal reported an impending cancer epidemic in India. As per their study, by 2020, 70% of those suffering from cancer worldwide will be located in developing countries, with one-fifth located in India. An analysis of cancer rates between the years 1982 and 2005 conducted by The Indian Council of Medical Research showed that 10 out of every 100,000 women living in Delhi, Mumbai, Chennai, and Bangalore were diagnosed with breast cancer about 10 years ago, compared with 23 women per every 100,000 today.

A few decades back, almost 60-70% of women suffering from breast cancer were above 50 years of age, and only 30-35% women were below fifty years of age.

Presently, breast cancer is more common in the younger age group and 53.2% of all women suffering from breast cancer in India are below 50 years of age. A significant number of patients are below 30 years of age too.

India is experiencing an unprecedented rise in the number of breast cancer cases across all sections of society, along with other countries. There is no way we can prevent breast cancer, but we can definitely detect it early and treat it adequately. More than half the patients still present themselves to doctors in advanced

---

[1] http://www.thelancet.com/journals/lancet/article/PIIS0140-6736%2812%2960415-2/fulltext

stages of the disease. Breast cancers in the young tend to be more aggressive than cancers in the older population, and survival in younger patients, especially in advanced stages, is lower.

Only and *only* with early detection can we achieve a longer survival. Since more patients in India turn up in later stages, they do not survive long in spite of the best treatment money can buy, and hence the mortality is fairly high.

There are many myths related to this disease, and this combined with a lack of awareness complicates the issue. Women do not know when is it that they need to see a doctor. They are also unaware as to which are the lumps in the breast that need immediate medical attention. Then, of course, women feel shy to talk about their breast, they hesitate to go to a male doctor and very often they waste their time taking alternative medicines. They fear that breast cancer is equal to removal of the breast and thus losing one's femininity.

The ignorance of some doctors also perpetuates the problem. There are cases where the patients present themselves on time, but doctors are unaware of the threat of breast cancer and delay treatment. Many doctors do not ask for the family history of breast cancer and do not ask the patient to undergo the necessary diagnostic tests for the same.

The social stigma associated with any cancer silences women. When more and more women talk about this disease in public, then the taboo may reduce, and women may become more aware and more open to receive the treatment. More awareness leads to better health and prompts timely treatment.

In India, the health of women is the last priority after that of men, children and elders. Women themselves hesitate to demand equitable health care. We lose thousands of young women annually to this patriarchal mindset.

No, I do not want my breast reconstructed

Divya was keen to know the progress in Ameena's health. The residual disease in Ameena's breast had slowly gripped everyone with a nagging anxiety. Ameena had been advised surgery. Unfortunately, her breast could not be saved. She had to undergo mastectomy (complete removal of the breast). She did not even want any reconstruction and instead she chose to wear an external prosthesis.

An external prosthesis is made up of silicon and can be slipped into the undergarment. It gives a shape exactly like that of a breast. This is a simple alternative to breast reconstruction surgeries, which some women prefer. This prosthesis was able to reinstate confidence in Ameena for her visible exterior. However, what I saw, as a doctor, was the tremendous strength that had filled this woman's interior!

Our hospital wanted to video-record Ameena's and her husband's success story. This kind of a video could help a lot of other women. I was very sceptical if she would agree. She never seemed to step out of her veil. But when she realised that it could help a lot of women, she along with her husband willingly agreed.

They spoke at length about their story and their ordeal. They also shared the hardships which they had endured, because of the political instability in their country. She was very grateful to our team and our hospital and most importantly, to our country. But she was sad that because of the prevailing unrest, she could not even invite us to her country. She, however, promised to keep us updated about her condition.

Before leaving, Ameena's husband wanted to know if they could have more children. To this, Ameena promptly answered, 'In that case, you can marry someone else.' He patted her affectionately and all of us had a hearty laugh. It just struck my mind that this timid, conservative lady had undergone a massive change in her personality in a matter of six months. She had developed immense self-confidence and could stand up for herself.

Divya also bid Ameena adieu with a heavy heart, but with a sense of satisfaction that her friend was going back home to her kids as a winner.

Meanwhile, Divya was very surprised to see a male patient in my OPD.

Yes, this disease could strike men as well. Though common in women, it is not rare in men. In fact, the incidence in men is increasing these days. Men need to be aware of their bodies as well. The treatment, however, is similar in men as in women.

Why delay?

It was always a new day at work. Even when we had predictably busy schedules, there was never any room for monotony. Every new patient, every new case history had so much learning to offer. Our out-patient clinic continued.

I saw a patient coming to our consultation in a wheel chair. She was breathless. Rajani was a forty-seven-year-old lady working in an MNC, holding a very senior post. She was a very smart, worldly wise, highly educated lady. Her work included meeting lots of clients and I was told that she was a kind of a counsellor for her entire family as well as for her friends, who came to her for various kinds of advice. Eight months ago, she had developed swelling and discomfort in the right hand. She had assumed it to be a menopausal symptom and water retention which is very common at that age.

Rajani had consulted a Homeopathy doctor who had treated her for six months. There was no relief, but she was told that the effect of the medicines would be only seen after a while. Subsequently, she developed rashes over her breast for which she further took treatment for a skin allergy from a dermatologist. This treatment lasted for another two months.

Suddenly, she became very breathless and was referred to our hospital. After examining her and after a few investigations, we concluded that she was suffering from an advanced stage of breast cancer. The cancer had spread extensively through her lungs, causing her breathlessness.

What was disturbing was the crucial time lost in getting the right diagnosis and starting definitive treatment.

She was immediately admitted in the ICU for further investigations and palliative treatment. Palliative treatment is given to patients who are in an advanced stage of breast cancer which has spread to distant parts of the body. Here, the emphasis is on improving the quality of life, without curative intent. In Rajani's case, it was given to relieve her breathlessness. Palliative treatment focuses on treating the symptoms and making the patient as comfortable as possible to lead a normal life.

Soon after Rajani, into our OPD came forty-five-year-old Deepa. She came from a small village near Gulbarga in Karnataka. She had never been to school. She was unmarried and lived with her old father and brother. Her world was her home as she had been confined to her house all her life.

When I examined her, I found that she had a big, fleshy growth in her left breast, which had protruded out of the skin, raw and red. I must admit that it was a ghastly sight. She had lived with this kind of a lump for more than a year. I was wondering how anyone could live with such a big mass – which would bleed when it touched any surface – without going for some treatment. She said that there was no female member in her family, so she was shy to share it with anyone and endured this for such a long time. It pained me to think that a woman goes through immense suffering quietly, even when medical facilities are not too inaccessible for her.

The day had started smoothly but ended up with a deep concern in my heart. Rajani and Deepa were both women of similar age and similar disease. Two women of different strata of society, one was educated and the other was not. One was part of the urban elite and the other was from a humble rural background. They both seemed so different, but was there really any difference between them? One was apparently negligent while the other was too shy to take timely treatment.

I wondered what the purpose of education is when it cannot make us wiser and help us prioritize our actions. What is the use of knowledge if it is not practically applied?

Every doctor wants to see their patients smile and get back to their lives after a complete cure. It is very painful to see women like Rajani and Deepa who lost out on the possibility of a complete cure due to misplaced inhibitions, negligence, ignorance and complacency.

I wish my hospital records were full of examples of women who get cured of the disease and bounce back to life. Doctors are known for their medical conversations. The stoic, medical jargon and cold autoclaved surgical instruments belie our soft interiors, our vulnerable hearts that feel compassion and invariably want to cure every patient that arrives ill to our examining room.

Life after cancer

My desk at the OPD is surrounded by informative graphic posters, thank you cards from patients and more. A weight management poster had particularly caught Divya's attention.

'Doctor, why are there so many posters in your outpatient clinic which suggest that we should maintain appropriate weight?' This was Divya's question.

It must be noted that maintaining a healthy weight is one thing that can be done to lower the life-time risk of breast cancer and its recurrence. Higher BMI (body mass index) can increase the risk of breast cancer and its recurrence by 30–60% (particularly worrisome is the often hidden abdominal fat). Physical activity reduces breast cancer risk and its recurrence. Exercising three or more hours per week could reduce the risk by 20– 30%.

A roundtable convened by the American College of Sports Medicine in 2010 reviewed available research and concluded that exercise is safe during and after all breast cancer treatments as long as you take any needed precautions and keep the intensity low. Exercise can lower the risk of breast cancer coming back, help one maintain a healthy weight, ease the side effects of the treatment and boost energy.

It improves physical functioning, quality of life, and cancer-related fatigue. There also is evidence that exercise can help breast cancer survivors live longer and lead a more active life.

Divya also wanted to know how Preeti had developed this disease when there was no relevant family history.

It is possible. Only about 30% of the women who develop breast cancer have a family history of the disease. The other 70% have what is called a 'sporadic occurrence' (without a known family history of the disease).

On whether the family members of patients be tested for cancer, it should be noted that some cancers like breast, prostate, pancreatic and colon can have a hereditary component. If someone in the family has one of these cancers, it may be advisable for other family members to undergo genetic testing. These genetic tests are now offered by many laboratories in India.

Divya also wanted to know why Ameena was given some tablets for ten years and she wasn't.

I explained that there are many subtypes of breast cancer. Some of the tumours are hormone dependent and some are not. The women who have tumours which are hormone dependent are the ones who receive hormone therapy. These are tablets which are given for a minimum of five years and some are given for ten years. Ameena was thus advised to take the tablet Tamoxifen for ten years.

Is a team necessary?

Sharing information is vital to every patient and doctor. Successful treatment is actually the result of team work and partnerships that exist not only between members of the medical team, but also between the patients, their families and the doctor.

Just like information and cooperation from patients is important, the decisions taken by the doctor can influence the outcome of treatment. Doctors need to do the right type of surgery; they need to take the correct decisions about radiation or chemotherapy. Even long-term follow-up and hormonal therapy determine the cure rates.

Hospitals need to establish well-equipped facilities. A well-trained and cohesive team of doctors, nurses, laboratories and other paramedical staff gives the patient the maximum chance of cure, not to mention comfort. Unfortunately, in our country, every other hospital and nursing home claims to do such surgeries, even though they may not be equipped to do so. Often the patient lands up with suboptimal results. Cancer treatment is a team work; it is a multi-modality treatment and needs to be treated in specialised centres. We need more such centres.

The inner peace

It has been one year since Divya finished her entire treatment. She had been coming for follow up regularly, once in three months. She seemed very happy as her PET CT showed that she was in complete remission. Her hair had grown; her nails and skin were back to normal. She had started her regular menstrual cycles. And she looked very beautiful. I knew the glow on her face was also due to the inner peace and the sublime knowledge that she had gained from this ordeal.

She had come with sweets for the entire ward staff. But she seemed to be lost in her thought, which she wanted to share with me.

'Doctor, this entire cancer treatment has been a life changing experience for me. I have learnt not to take anything or anybody for granted. I have started valuing everything around me. I am grateful to my family, my friends, and the opportunities that I have got in my life. I have learnt the value of gratitude. I have learnt to accept things that cannot be changed. I feel one will find peace not by trying to escape problems, but by confronting them courageously. Peace can be found, not in denial, but in victory. I appreciate the peace that acceptance can bring into life. When I accept what cannot be changed, new avenues open up for life to ascend to new heights. We ourselves do not know how strong we are until being strong is the only choice we have.'

We both agreed that after all, our health is our responsibility. Another responsible thing to do is to have an adequate medical insurance. I think it can be one of the best investments one could do for their own family. When faced with a medical issue, at least if finances are taken care of, it can bring down the stress to a great extent.

Couldn't we have prevented it? Could we have detected it earlier?

ᴙ

She seemed to be introspecting.

'Doctor, can breast cancer be prevented?' she asked.

I said, 'This is a question which a lot of women ask me. Certain factors can surely bring down the risk of developing breast cancer. These are maintaining optimal weight of the body, regular exercises, having the first child before thirty years of age, and breast feeding each child. If certain reproductive hormone, e.g. estrogen, progesterone tablets (such as menstrual regulation or contraceptive pills) have to be taken, they should be taken only under medical supervision. However, there are many factors which are not in our control like the genes that we inherit, ageing, and being a woman. Breast cancer cannot be prevented in the true sense; it can only be detected early. Early detection is the key for success.

There are early detection guidelines. If these are followed regularly, then the chances of detecting a lump in the breast early are very high. Early detection is through 'Breast Cancer Screening'. A screening test is done routinely for people who appear to be healthy and are not suspected of having breast cancer. Their purpose is to find breast cancer early, before any symptoms can develop. The cancer thus diagnosed usually is easier to treat.

Breast self-examination should be a part of the monthly health care routine, and a woman should visit the doctor if she experiences breast changes. The earlier breast cancer is found and diagnosed, the better are the chances of beating it.

All women who are twenty years old and above should do breast self-examination once a month. Since breasts are often painful or sensitive just before the periods, it is recommended that they do this test on the seventh day of the periods. They can do it on any particular date of the month, even if they have irregular periods, have had a hysterectomy (removal of the uterus), or have already reached menopause.

Women who are twenty to forty years of age should go to a doctor and get breast examination done once in three years.

Women, who are forty years and above, in addition, should undergo a mammogram once in a year. This is a method by which a breast lump can be detected, when it is so small in size that it cannot even be felt by the hands. It could even be just a few millimetres in size. If treatment is given at this stage, the chances of complete cure are very high.

With breast cancer, there's a misconception that if you feel fine, don't have a lump, and have no family history of breast cancer, you're okay. The truth is that three-quarters of the women who develop breast cancer have no risk factors. So screening is important for everyone.

There can be life after breast cancer. The prerequisite is early detection.

Your age group	Which examination?	How frequently?
20- 40 years	Clinical (CBE)	Once in 3 years
	Self (BSE)	Once a month
Above 40 years	Mammogram & Clinical CBE	Once a year
	Self (BSE)	Once a month

However, some women are at a greater risk of developing this disease. The risk factors are :

- First degree relatives with breast /ovarian cancer
- BRCA 1/BRCA 2 mutation and others
- Untested first degree relative of known carrier
- Chest radiation at a young age

Screening for women at high risk

Breast self examination once a month for all women above 20 years:

- Clinical breast examination at least once in a year
- Mammography/ Breast MRI from age 25 years (Genetic test BRCA 1 and 2 detected positive)
- 10 years earlier than the age of affected first degree relative with premenopausal disease

She suddenly seemed enlightened; her eyes suddenly seemed to light up with excitement. She seemed to have a brain wave. Being more informed and confident, she bid me goodbye.

Who is she?

Promptly, I received a mail from Divya at night. She seemed to have chalked out a complete plan for the STHREE organisation (STHREE is an organisation which Supports to Heal, Restore, Empower and Energize patients who are undergoing treatment for breast cancer). She felt, while everyone's journey is unique, knowing that others before you have been through something similar can give you the strength and inspiration you need to keep everything in perspective.

She wrote, 'Cancer woke me up to my health, and I feel like I have been given a second chance.'

She was willing to lead the organisation. Divya seemed very confident that there were many women amongst the cancer survivors who had become her friends during the course of her treatment, and were ready to volunteer for different kinds of activities. She mentioned that these survivors could counsel the new patients. She suggested that they could go through a formal course in counselling. Their life experiences combined with formal training in counselling can equip them to be very effective counsellors.

She had planned that there could be some volunteers who could also do the awareness programmes. She requested the doctors to train these women. She named the awareness programme as 'Lump to laughter'. Her aim is that every woman who develops a lump in the breast has a happy conclusion. She feels no woman should die because of breast cancer, which is so treatable. Every woman needs to know the facts. And the fact is – when it comes to breast cancer, every woman is at risk. Her message to every woman was: 'The only person who can save you is *you*.'

It was so heartening to read her mail. She seemed to have found a new purpose for her life.

It has been several years since she completed her treatment for breast cancer. My heart is filled with joy whenever I hear her sing the theme song of STHREE, a poem by Rabindranath Tagore from his book *Gitanjali*.

Where the mind is without fear

ꭕ

Where the mind is without fear and the head is held high,
Where knowledge is free, where the world is not broken into fragments
By narrow domestic walls,
Where words come out from the depth of truth,
Where tireless striving stretches its arms towards perfection,
Where the clear stream of reason has not lost its way
Into the dreary desert sand of dead habit,
Where the mind is led forward by thee
Into ever-widening thought and action
Into that heaven of freedom, my Father, let my country awake.

– Rabindranath Tagore, *Gitanjali*

Together we can make a world, where cancer no longer means living with fear and without hope. If I leave this earth, I want to leave knowing I've tried to give something back and tried to do something worthwhile with myself.

Every time I see her taking the lead and organising all the STHREE activities, I understand that she is not only a woman who has reinvented a new self, she is also a brand ambassador for courage and hope; she is not only someone who is selflessly spreading awareness and educating women, she is also a source of inspiration for many people; not only is she someone who met cancer in her chest, humbled it and moved on to be known as a cancer survivor, but she is

a true woman of substance.

FAQs

Q1) I have a lump in my breast and I am afraid it is cancer. Should I be worried?

A) As many as 80% of the women who feel lumps in their breast have benign lumps (not cancerous). About 20% of the women could have malignant lumps (cancerous) in their breast. A benign lump can be a collection of normal or hyperactive breast gland cells, or maybe a water filled sac (cyst) and it does not have cancer

If you feel a lump and you are worried, do not hesitate to see a doctor. It will ease your fears and if it is something serious, you can start treatment immediately.

Q2) What is breast cancer?

A) Breast cancer is the collective term for all the cancers that originate in the breast tissue. Breast cancer is a disease in which malignant (cancer) cells form in the tissue of the breast.

Q3) What are the warning signs?

The commonest signs of breast cancer are:

a) Lump or thickening in the breast
b) Change in the size or shape of the breast

c) Discharge from the nipple
d) Change in the colour or feel of the skin of the breast or nipple (dimpled, puckered, scaly, warm, red or swollen)
e) Nipple turning inwards
f) Lump in the under arm area

There may be no warning signs or symptoms. Breast self examination, clinical breast examination, and regular mammogram are essential for early detection of breast cancer.

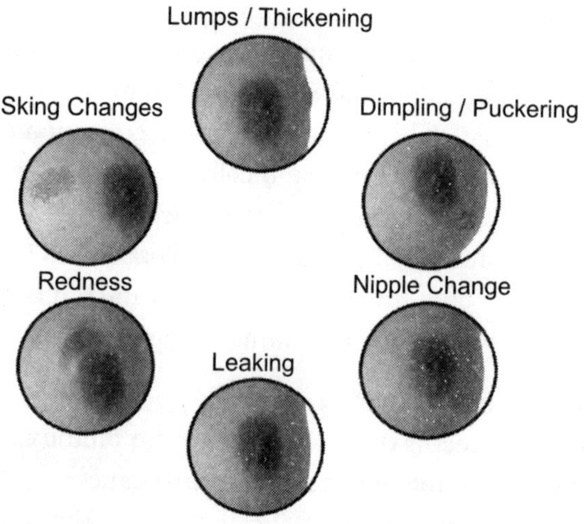

Figure 13: Signs and symptoms of breast cancer.

Q4) What are my risks for getting breast cancer?

Being a woman and getting older are the biggest risk factors.

Others being:

a) Onset of menstruation before 12 years of age
b) Menopause after 50 years of age

c) Not having children or having a first child after age 30
d) Family history of breast cancer
e) Obesity
f) Alcohol consumption
g) Using hormone replacement therapy or birth control pills
h) Not breastfeeding children

Q5) **How does weight influence breast cancer and can exercise really help to cut down the risk of breast cancer?**

A) Maintaining a healthy weight is one thing that can be done to lower the life-time risk of breast cancer. Higher BMI (body mass index) can increase the risk of breast by 30-60% (particularly worrisome is the often hidden abdominal fat).

Physical activity reduces breast cancer risk. Exercising three or more hours per week could reduce the risk by 20 to 30%.

Q6) **If no one in my family has breast cancer, can I still get it?**

A) Yes, you still can. Only about 30% of women who develop breast cancer have a family history of the disease. The other 70% have what is called a 'sporadic occurrence' (without a known family history of the disease)

Q7) **When should I start having mammograms and how often should I have them?**

A) Women from the age of forty years onward should have a mammogram done yearly. The younger women typically have dense breasts and on a mammogram, this dense breast shows up as white – which is the same colour, that cancer appears as on mammogram. As the woman ages, the dense tissue in the woman's breast is replaced with fatty tissue which looks grey on a mammogram. It is much easier to see the white cancer against this grey background. Mammogram can help you find your cancer early.

Q8) Is a mammogram painful?

A) The pressure caused by compressing and stretching the breast tissue maybe uncomfortable, but not painful.

Q9) Is the radiation exposure from getting a mammogram harmful?

A) The radiation exposure from low dose, modern mammography machines is minimal. Radiation doses usually are so low that they are negligible. The medical benefits of early detection outweigh any potential risk.

Q10) How is breast cancer diagnosed?

A) When you are referred to a specialised breast centre, physical examination and some tests will be organised to determine if you have breast cancer. These tests are:

a) Mammogram

b) Ultrasound/ MRI breast

c) Biopsy – a small sample of breast tissue is removed using a needle on an outpatient basis. The result of biopsy is available within 3 or 4 days.

Q11) How does breast cancer spread?

A Breast cancer cells can break away from the original site and move around the body to form secondary breast cancer. This spread usually occurs via blood and lymphatics. Lymph nodes in the arm pit are a common place for breast cancer to spread. Such spread can happen to some of the distant organs like liver, lungs, bones, brain, etc.

Q12) How do I decide which treatment option is best for me?

A) Your physician will discuss the various treatment options available. Although there are four standard ways to treat breast cancer – surgery, chemotherapy, radiation therapy, hormonal therapy – several treatments may be combined. Your doctor will recommend a treatment depending on the type and location of cancer, the stage at which it is detected, your age, and general health condition.

Q13) How do I decide which surgery is right for me?

A) Two main types of surgery are used in treatment of breast cancer.

First is the breast conservation surgery, also known as lumpectomy. Only the cancerous lump in the breast and a small amount of surrounding normal tissue is removed. Rest of the breast tissue is left intact.

The second is the mastectomy. Whole of the affected breast is operated and removed.

Your surgeon will decide the type of surgery most suitable for you, considering a number of factors like the size and location of the tumour within the breast.

Women who undergo breast conservation surgery will require radiation therapy after surgery. Radiation therapy reduces the chances of tumour recurring in the breast.

Q14) Is it necessary to undergo an operation to remove the glands from the arm pit?

A) The most common site for breast cancer cells to spread is to the small glands called lymph nodes in the arm pit. Their removal is done through a procedure known as sentinel lymph node biopsy or axillary lymph node dissection. This is normally performed at the same time as removal of the breast tumour or complete breast. This procedure helps us in planning the further treatment like chemotherapy and radiation therapy.

Q15) If I have a mastectomy, does that mean I won't need any other treatment after surgery?

A) No. In some cases, after mastectomy it may still be necessary to undergo radiotherapy, chemotherapy and hormonal therapy, depending on the type of the tumour and the stage of the disease.

Q16) What are the side effects of the treatment?

A) **Chemotherapy-**

The side effects of chemotherapy are different for different people. This also depends on the different kinds of drugs and drug doses which are used. The side effects of chemotherapy are listed as follows, though not everyone will experience all the side effects:

a) Nausea and vomiting
b) Hair loss
c) Fatigue
d) Anaemia
e) Mouth sores
f) Diarrhoea
g) Cessation of menstruation, temporary or permanent
h) Infertility

Radiotherapy-

Fibrosis or scarring of the remaining breast tissue may occur following radiotherapy. In some cases, the breast can become noticeably smaller and harder. Fibrosis can also block lymph drainage of the arm and cause swelling of the arm.

Hormonal therapy-

The side effects are similar to symptoms experienced by women who are going through menopause, such as hot flushes, night sweats, vaginal dryness, irregular periods, and in some cases joint pain.

Q17) **Should my family members be tested for cancer?**

A) Some cancers like breast, prostate, pancreatic and colon can have a hereditary component. If someone in the family has one of these cancers, it may be advisable for other family members to undergo genetic testing.

Q18) **Will my cancer come back?**

A) This is one of the most common questions asked by cancer survivors. In some cases, cancer can recur or a new cancer can form years or even decades after treatment. One of the goals of breast cancer support group is to help patients come to terms with their fears about cancer recurrence, so that they can lead a productive and fulfilling life. Another goal is to ensure that the survivors realize the importance of periodic check-ups after their last treatment for cancer.

Breast awareness and self-exam

What is a breast self-exam?

The breast self-exam is a way through which you can check your breasts for changes (such as lumps or thickenings). It includes looking at and feeling your breast. Any unusual changes should be reported to your doctor. When breast cancer is detected in its early stages, your chances of surviving the disease are greatly improved.

Beginning in their twenties, women should be told about the benefits and limitations of breast self-exam (BSE). Finding a breast change does not necessarily mean there is a cancer.

A woman can notice changes by knowing how her breasts normally look and feel and feeling her breasts for changes (breast awareness), or by choosing to use a step-by-step approach (with a BSE) and using a specific schedule to examine her breasts.

Women who are pregnant or breastfeeding can also choose to examine their breasts regularly.

The following information provides a step-by-step approach for the exam. The best time for a woman to examine her breasts is when they are not tender or swollen.

How to examine your breasts

Step 1: Begin by looking at your breasts in the mirror with your shoulders straight and your arms on your hips.

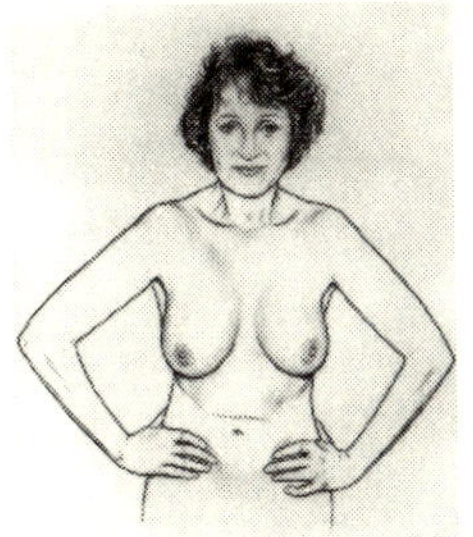

Here's what you should look for:

- Breasts that are their usual size, shape, and colour
- Breasts that are evenly shaped without visible distortion or swelling

If you see any of the following changes, bring them to your doctor's attention:

- Dimpling, puckering, or bulging of the skin
- A nipple that has changed position or an inverted nipple (pushed inward instead of sticking out)
- Redness, soreness, rash, or swelling

Step 2: Now, raise your arms and look for the same changes.

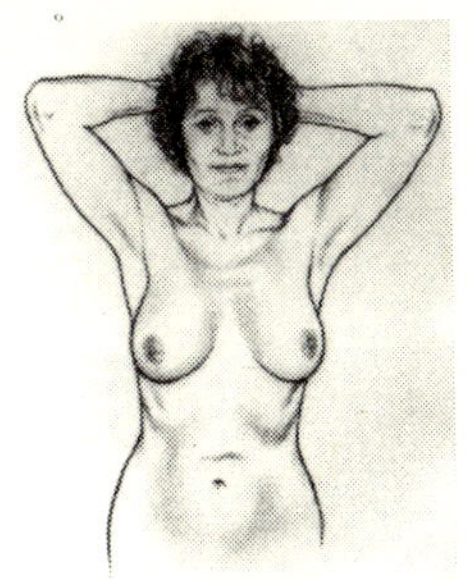

Step 3: While you're at the mirror, look for any signs of fluid coming out of one or both nipples (this could be a watery, milky, or yellow fluid or blood).

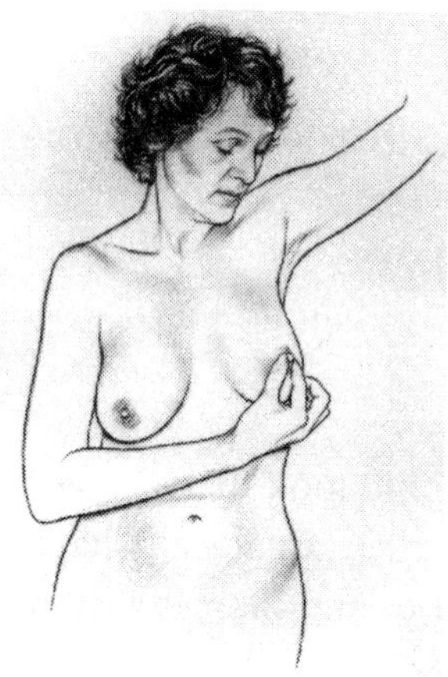

Step 4: Feel your breasts while you are standing or sitting. Many women find that the easiest way to feel their breasts is when their skin is wet and slippery, so they like to do this step in the shower. Cover your entire breast, using the hand movements.

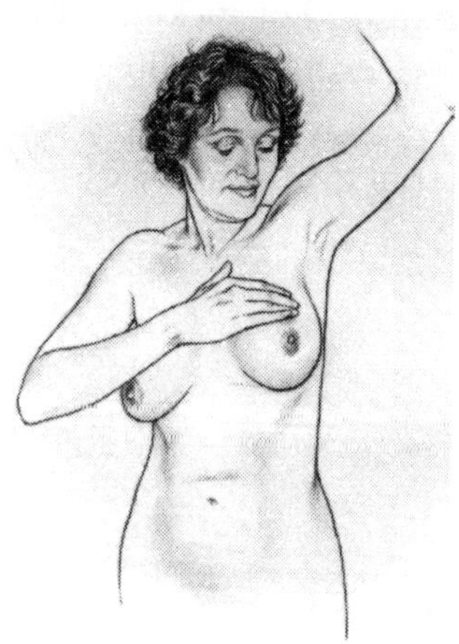

Step 5: Next, feel your breasts while lying down, using your right hand to feel your left breast and then your left hand to feel your right breast. Use a firm, smooth touch with the first few finger pads of your hand, keeping the fingers flat and together. Use a circular motion, about the size of a quarter.

Cover the entire breast from top to bottom, side to side; from your collarbone to the top of your abdomen, and from your armpit to your cleavage.

Follow a pattern to be sure that you cover the whole breast. You can begin at the nipple, moving in larger and larger circles until you reach the outer edge of the breast. You can also move your fingers up and down vertically, in rows, as if you were mowing a lawn. This up-and-down approach seems to work best for most women. Be sure to feel all the tissue from the front to the back of your breasts: for the skin and tissue just beneath, use light pressure; use medium pressure for tissue in the middle of your breasts; use firm pressure for the deep tissue in the back. When you've reached the deep tissue, you should be able to feel down to your ribcage.

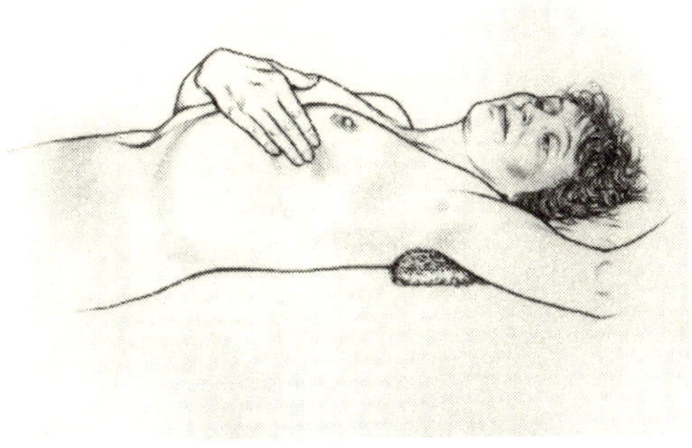

Cancer Survivors Speak

A story of hope

Kamaldeep Peter

Writing this piece has taken longer than I thought. I am not sure if this will be of any interest or of value to anyone. Yet I have put this together to reach out to those who are to dwell on the misfortune of fighting cancer. This would be a small packet of hope to those who are battling breast cancer in the month of the pink ribbon.

It was 24 February 2013, a Sunday around 11.00 a.m. I was sipping steaming coffee in a CCD outlet and my mind was brewing with worrisome thoughts. The mammogram technician across the road insisted that I came back for an ultrasound and the doctor would be certainly coming in. Her insistence and my health condition for nearly a year confirmed that an intruder was playing havoc in my body. All that was needed was a formal printed report which I received the same day. I did not try to learn the name of this young mammogram technician, but to this day, I thank her for her insistence to have me back. But for her, I would have boarded the flight that night to San Francisco to attend a team meeting with the rest of the tests waiting for my return.

Everything that happened thereafter was very typical. Family was making rounds of hospitals seeking second opinion, going in for more confirmatory tests, finding the best doctor in the city. Thankfully, we quickly decided to have my treatment done at the BGS Global Hospital, Bangalore. I must admit that the hospital has an amazing team of oncologists, nursing staff and support team who instil confidence and hope in you. The fitness tests were swiftly completed and I was wheeled out of the operation theatre on 1st March with the cancerous mass removed. Time is a crucial factor in determining how successful the battle with cancer is. An early diagnosis makes cancer not only treatable, but also curable.

Many women like me are kind of insane for we can't figure out what is good for us. We never know what duty hours are and clock each minute with selflessness at home and at work place. It is only when you are pronounced of any major illness that you are repentant of not heeding the early signals and warnings that the human body sends to the conscious being.

It says: "Discipline and Act immediately!"

Troubled, conflicted and despaired I was, like never before. But further overdue concern of the dilemma of why I was chosen would only make things worse. I resolved to put aside memories of two of my close friends losing their battle to cancer, and move away from people who made me believe that cancer was cataclysmic. I actually wanted to live on for I felt I had still unfinished business in this world, more as a mother. The irony was that if I was not too young to crave for life, I was neither too old to die. I had turned fifty, three years back.

In the fight with cancer, there is little place for self-pity. I had to steel and fortify myself for the eight chemotherapies and thirty-three radiations, for my report said that the disease was in stage 3. I heeded every word the team of doctors had to say. One profound statement that helped my treatment remain on track was: "Keep yourself away from infections or else we would spend more time treating your infection rather than treating cancer".

The effect of chemotherapy sweeps you off your senses and feet. A total devastation rips through your body and you are asked to repair it quickly to have your next cycle of chemotherapy. How can you eat when you can hardly digest food? How difficult it is to expect someone to give you freshly cooked food every few hours for six months? What it means to be discussed in low voices about your physical appearance when you have lost your tresses and eyebrows?

At such a time, I took deep refuge in my work, both official and domestic. It helped me establish self-worth and an assurance that I can do everything, if not more than a healthy person, of course interspersed with brief periods of rest. I just took a couple of days off around chemotherapy and kept myself deeply immersed in work, not with a feeling of being indispensable, but with a fear of getting dependent on others.

Confidence and gratitude were a very important part of my life and to this I now added a high dose of positive thoughts. I am ever grateful to God for helping me decide to go ahead for the medical coverage scheme a few years earlier and giving me the support of family and friends. Today in the first line of thoughts, I strongly recommend each one of you reading this piece to get every member of the family medically insured.

Almost one year has passed and I have survived cancer! I return regularly to my doctors, not only for medical check-ups, but also to extend my help to those who are battling cancer or have survived the ordeal but are fighting a sense of loneliness and fear.

Interestingly, a close friend of mine asked me a very profound question just a couple of days back.

Can a cancer survivor contribute as much as before? My answer to this is in the words of G.K. Chesterton. "The true soldier fights not because he hates what is in front of him, but because he loves what is behind him."

Feel free to reach me with your comments and queries at kamaldeep.peter@gmail.com.

A brush with breast cancer

Yeshi Dolker

I was not unaware of breast cancer. I knew about it. I knew about the importance of early diagnoses. I knew about self-examinations and I knew about the importance of annual checkups after forty. But for various reasons, I kept putting off check-ups. However, I continued with self-examinations. It had become a practice for nearly three decades that I had actually become very familiar with every lump in my breast.

One afternoon, I felt an unusual thickening in my breast. It was unlike any that I had felt before. I was in the midst of my pre-menopausal stage and my periods had become irregular. So although I was a little anxious, I brushed it aside as one of those hardenings just before a period. I gave myself more than a week, hoping that it would go away on its own. But to my utter dismay, it didn't! I instinctively knew that something was seriously wrong. Filled with fear, I told my husband about it and we went immediately to the nearest cancer hospital – BGS Global.

It was at this hospital that I met my doctor, Dr. Jayanti S Thumsi, Senior Breast Cancer Consultant and Surgeon for the first time in my life. She was a young, energetic and unassuming woman. There was an air of confidence and calmness about her that could have only come from experience. I felt at ease. I later also read about her and was indeed glad to know that I was in very good hands.

She walked me through the whole process carefully and patiently (mammogram, ultra sound and biopsy) and assured me that everything will be fine. What made me further feel good about this hospital was the accuracy and the speed at which the test results came out – something that would have taken ages many years ago even in the best of hospitals.

The next day, I went back to the hospital for the diagnoses. I tried to keep myself composed all the while but prepared to hear the worst. My doctor finally broke the bad news to me. My heart sank. I was cold, unable to think clearly. I felt a sense of helplessness like never before. I felt like I was being sucked into this gaping hole and could do nothing about it. Slowly, I regained sense and I recall having all sorts of feelings. First a sense of disbelief and anger – why me when nobody in my family had had it – and then a sense of fear of the uncertain.

But my doctor seemed least perturbed. She explained to me with such calmness and confidence and with a lot of positivity about the best treatment available. This gave me hope and made me see things in a whole new light. I was all ready to start treatment – surgery (lumpectomy), chemotherapy and radiotherapy.

Chemo was what I dreaded the most. I had heard horrible stories about it. I had heard that it was a 'healing hell'. But with the information that I got from my doctors, from the web and from two cancer survivors, I knew exactly what to expect. And to my pleasant surprise, I found that it was not as bad as it sounded. Except for some mild side effects, I had no complications at all. And this obviously was all because of the new medications that helped control the side effects.

It was only after going through a few cycles of chemo that I noticed that chemo had a cumulative effect. I found that the side effects were different during different cycles even though the drugs were the same. Why didn't I know about it! How could I have missed that! Not anticipating it caused some confusion and frustration because I was completely in the dark. But being proactive in spite of this helped me understand it and deal with it. For example, in my second cycle I experienced a coldness that severely disturbed my sleep for a few days. But I searched the web and was able to find information on how to manage it. In addition, I also experienced sleeplessness which was itself a side effect of chemo. This was horrible because it made me think of negative thoughts, keeping me more awake and completely depressed and fatigued. Once again, I looked for solutions. My husband brought me books and videos on conscious breathing meditation as a way to calm my mind. And this worked wonders for me.

However, unlike many women, losing my hair to chemo was the least of my worries. I knew it was temporary. Besides, I always thought it was fashionable to be bald. I didn't want to wear a wig because it felt so unnatural. Instead, I tried all kinds of colourful head-wraps and beautiful earrings and I truly enjoyed the experience!

I realized that maintaining a positive frame of mind was so important for me to cope with the disease and the medications. So throughout the treatment, I kept myself occupied with activities that I always wanted to do, but didn't really have the time to develop. I engaged myself in gardening, cooking, walking, meditation, reading and writing. It gave me a sense of freedom and happiness I had never experienced before.

But I would not have been able to cope so well without the support of my husband. With my daughters and relatives, all living abroad, my only support was my husband. He was everything to me. He cooked, he washed, he did the shopping, he accompanied me to the hospital and he even went to work. He bore it all with such strength and positivity that rubbed off on me and also gave me a sense of security that was so crucial to my road to recovery.

Cancer changed my life completely. It has made me calmer, stronger, more level-headed and more proactive. Also, today I live with a mindfulness I never did before. But the most important change is that it brought me and my husband closer. We understand each other better and we love each other...more than we ever did!

Opportunity Lost

Anant Kumar

It was a beautiful day on 14 April 2010. It was a typical Wednesday morning. My wife Namitha was busy in the kitchen and my daughters were in a hurry to leave for college. I was sipping coffee with a newspaper in my hand. I was enjoying my retired life and the freedom I had just acquired since two months.

My wife was rushing to the office after finishing the household chores. I fondly looked at her as she waved me goodbye. She promised to return from work by 7.00 p.m. and then we could plan for our upcoming holiday to Singapore.

I could not thank god enough for the beautiful family that I had. I felt most fortunate to have such a loving wife. Everything seemed to be so beautiful, almost like a fairy tale. But of course, nothing lasts forever...neither the good times nor the bad ones.

Namitha looked distressed on returning from work. She had attended an awareness programme in her office about breast cancer. Thereby she was coaxed by her friends to be examined by the doctor who was visiting their office. She reluctantly underwent breast examination. The doctor had found a lump in her breast. She advised her to get further investigations done immediately.

Namitha had fear in her eyes and anxiety in her mind. I immediately took my car out and went to the nearest diagnostic centre to get her mammogram done. The events followed one after the other. Our fear had come true. Namitha was diagnosed to have breast cancer.

She was advised immediate surgery. Namitha was counselled to undergo breast conservation surgery. Being beauty conscious, she was happy that she did not have to get complete removal of her breast. Surgery and post surgical period was uneventful. The final biopsy report was very favourable. There was no trace of disease left in her breast.

Being stage 2 disease, she was advised chemotherapy followed by radiation therapy. We were told that only on completion of the treatment, chances of cure were very high

Namitha was confused. She argued, 'If the disease was completely removed surgically, then where is the need for further treatment?' As a family we cajoled, begged and pleaded her to complete her treatment. She was worried about the hair loss; she had some misconceptions about chemotherapy as well. She vehemently refused chemotherapy.

No amount of convincing, either from the doctors or the family and friends helped. Namitha stubbornly stuck to her point.

She began to work post surgery. Her hectic life restarted. She seemed very confident with herself and her decision, to an extent that at times I found her to be arrogant.

She was fine but for a few episodes of tiredness which she linked to her ageing process.

Things went on smoothly but I always had a sense of impending doom.

Two years later, Namitha was getting ready for her own retirement function. While bathing, she noticed a lump in the same breast.

We immediately rushed to the doctor. The disease had promptly come back.

PET-CT scan showed that the disease had spread to her lungs and liver as well. The doctors told us that the disease which had been in stage 2 had progressed to stage 4 because of incomplete treatment. She was advised chemotherapy, but with only palliative, not curative intent. The disease which had a high chance of complete cure if treated completely had advanced to a stage where cure was impossible.

Cancer is hard to go through, but it is even harder to see someone you love go through it.

Namitha took two cycles of chemotherapy and then died.

I couldn't stop crying. I had to pay a price for her foolishness. I am amazed by the human attitude.

How has education helped women like my wife? Is the external beauty so dear that women are blind to the implications it could have on their life? Is there no value for the medical research and the enormous efforts that have gone into it for the betterment of mankind? Doctors had advised her to follow evidence based medicine which has scientific basis of research in millions and millions of women from all over the world. But Namitha had chosen a path of ignorance and audacity.

Some people call it *destiny*, but I prefer to call it *human stupidity.*

Opportunity lost.

List of figures

ጸ

References

ᴪ

1. For data for 2005-2009: Office for National Statistics (ONS). *Cancer survival in England: Patients diagnosed 2005-2009 and followed up to 2010*. London: ONS; 2011.
2. For data for 2007: Coleman MP, et al. *Research commissioned by Cancer Research UK, London School of Hygiene and Tropical Medicine*. 2010.
3. For data for 2001-2003 Office for National Statistics (ONS). *Cancer survival rates, Long-term Breast Cancer Survival, England and Walves*. London: ONS; 2005.
4. Welsh Cancer Intelligence and Surveillance Unit (WCISU). *Cancer Survival Trends in Wales 1985-2004*. Cardiff: WCISU; 2010.
5. Information Services Division Scotland (ISD Scotland). *Cancer Statistics. Cancer of the Breast*. Accessed September 2011.
6. Northern Ireland Cancer Registry (NICR). *Cancer Survival Online Statistics. Breast*. Accessed September 2011.
7. Mathew A, Pandey M, Rajan B. *Do younger women with non-metastatic and non-inflammatory breast carcinoma have poor prognosis?* World J Surg Oncol. 2004; 2(1):2.
8. Chia KS, Du WB, Sankaranarayanan R, et al. *Do younger female breast cancer patients have a poorer prognosis? Results from a population-based survival analysis*. Int J Cancer 2004;108(5):761-765.

9. NHS *Breast Screening Programme.*
10. Department of Health. *Improving outcomes: a strategy for cancer.* London: Department of Health; 2011.
11. For data for 1971-1990: Coleman MP, Babb P, Damiecki P, et al. *Cancer Survival Trends in England and Wales,* 1971-1995: Deprivation and NHS Region. Series SMPS No 61. London: ONS; 1999.
12. For data for 1991-1995: Office for National Statistics (ONS). *Cancer Survival: England and Wales, 1991-2001, twenty major cancers by age group.* London: ONS; 2005.
13. For data for 1996-2003: Rachet B, Maringe C, Nur U, et al. *Population-based cancer survival trends in England and Wales up to 2007.* Lancet Oncol 2009;10:351-369. Age-standardised figures were provided by the author on request.
14. *Cancer Research UK. Cancer Stats report. Survival – England and Wales.* London: Cancer Research UK; 2004.
15. http://www.breastcancer.org/symptoms/testing/types/self_exam/bse_steps
16. http://www.cancer.org/cancer/breastcancer/moreinformation/breastcancerearlydetection/breast-cancer-early-detection-acs-recs-bse
17. http://www.ncbi.nlm.nih.gov/pubmed/22987302
18. http://www.ncbi.nlm.nih.gov/pubmed/22459198
19. http://www.breastcancerindia.net/statistics/stat_global.html
20. seer.cancer.gov/statfacts/html/breast.html
21. Cancer of the Breast - SEER Stat Fact Sheets
22. Incidence/mortality data: Ferlay J, Soerjomataram I, Ervik M, Dikshit R, Eser S, Mathers C, Rebelo M, Parkin DM, Forman D, Bray, F (2013). GLOBOCAN 2012 v1.0, Cancer Incidence and Mortality Worldwide: IARC CancerBase No. 11 [Internet]. Lyon, France: International Agency for Research on Cancer. Available from http://globocan.iarc.fr. Prevalence data: Bray F,

Ren JS, Masuyer E, Ferlay J (2013). Global estimates of cancer prevalence for 27 sites in the adult population in 2008. Int J Cancer, 132(5):1133–1145. http://dx.doi.org/10.1002/ijc.27711 PMID:22752881

23. http://www.thelancet.com/journals/lancet/article/PIIS0140-6736%2812%2960415-2/fulltext
24. http://www.icmr.nic.in/
25. http://seer.cancer.gov/statfacts/html/breast.htm
26. http://globocan.iarc.fr/old/burden.asp?selection_pop=89356&Text-p=India&selection_cancer=3152&Text-c=Breast&pYear=3&type=0&window=1&submit=%C2%A0Execute